SHACKLEBOUND BOOKS

Dread Space

First published by Shacklebound Books 2022

First edition

Editing by Eric Fomley

This book was professionally typeset on Reedsy.
Find out more at reedsy.com

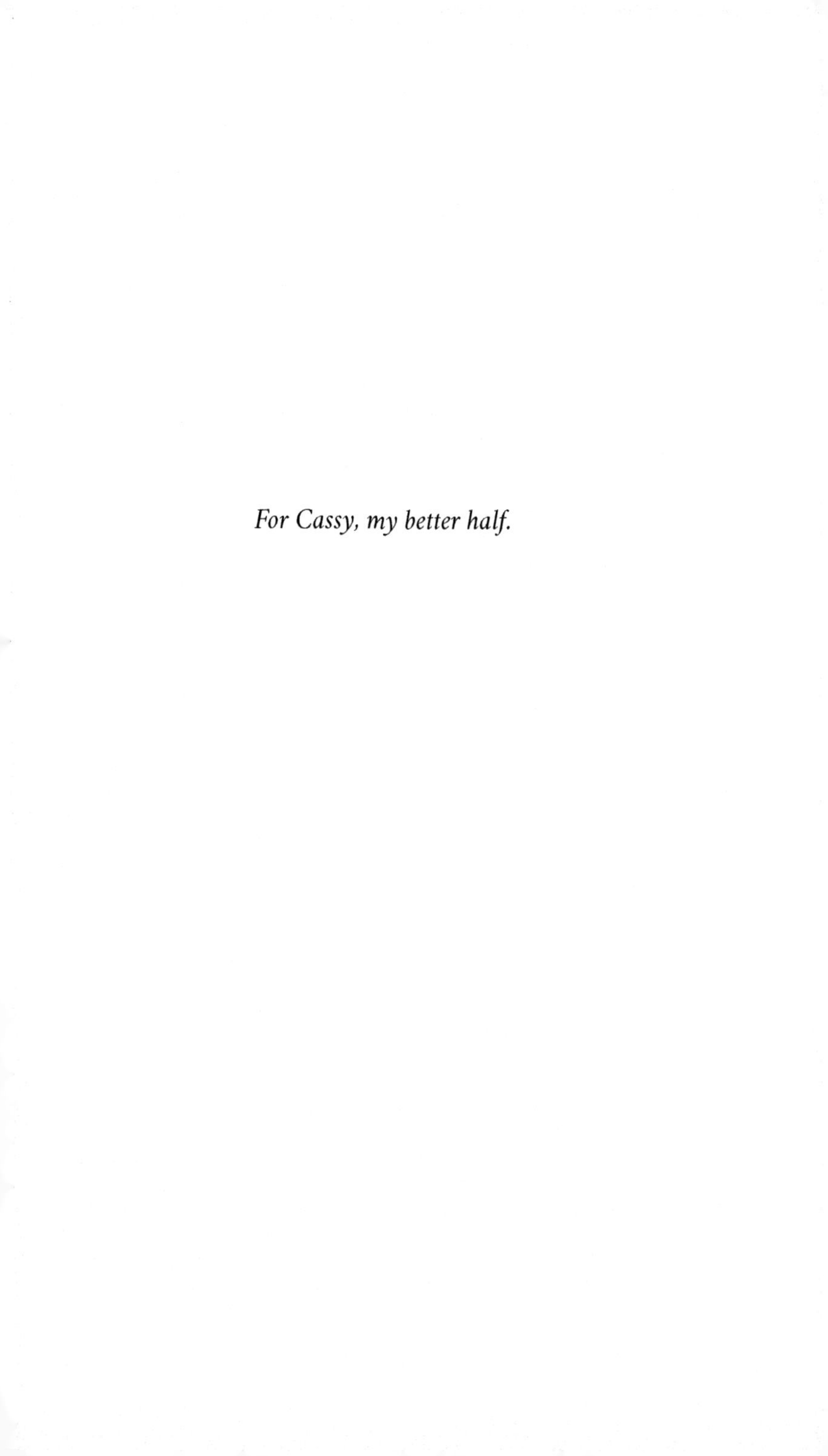

For Cassy, my better half.

Contents

This Is the Genesis Ship Arkhaven by Jonathan Ficke

"This is the Genesis Ship, *Arkhaven*," a garbled transmission crackled over the speakers on the bridge. "Identify yourself, over."

The fact that the massive ship only visible as a gleaming speck of high albedo mass from his bridge was identifying itself as the very ship that Captain Matthew "Sully" Sullivan commanded was disconcerting. The fact that it was on a collision course with his own—a fact that the alarm klaxons blaring across the bridge would not stop alerting him to—raised the situation from frustrating prank to life-or-death problem.

The *Arkhaven* was designed for two purposes, first to build a Krasnikov Bridge enabling superluminal transit to a habitable star, and second to be the vanguard of humanity to the stars. It was a technological Noah's Ark containing enough life—human, animal, and vegetable—to sustain a foothold on an extrasolar planet. Sully simply could not allow whatever it was that was masquerading with his callsign to snuff out the lives in his charge with its unrestrained burn trajectory.

"Your window for a missile launch is closing." Commander Daluxo's dark uniform was as crisp as it would be before any inspection. Unlike some attached to the *Arkhaven* mission who coped with the certainty of never returning to Earth with minute lapses in discipline, Daluxo never flagged with even the tiniest details. "We need to launch, or we need to leave."

"Are we ready to leave? Is the cargo secure? The Krasnikov Engine primed?"

"Every last embryo." Daluxo said, his fingers drumming against a digital timer counting down the time until the calculations suggested a missile strike would merely create a cloud of debris that would destroy the *Arkhaven* in a rain of small impacts rather than a single catastrophic one. "The Engine is... lacking its final test, but every simulation agrees that it's ready."

"Open a channel." Sully waited for the telltale click in his earpiece that denoted an open frequency. "*This* is the Genesis Ship, *Arkhaven*. Identify yourself, over."

"Captain." Daluxo rose from his console took his place by Sully's side. "That's us."

Though the shining speck grew larger with every second, Sully looked from the viewport to the screen where Daluxo was pointing at an optical scan. The ship on a hard burn for them was identical to the *Arkhaven*.

Sweat beaded on Daluxo's brow and his lip trembled. "Captain, the timer. We need to launch now."

Sully lifted his fingers to tent them over his mouth. How could the ship on his scan be the ship on which he stood? He needed to protect the *Arkhaven*, and it took only one simple word and a missile to do so. All it would cost was... what exactly? Seven million human lives frozen and waiting to be incubated to take their place ensuring the lifeboat of human civilization? Were those lives even still aboard the phantom bearing down on them? How was any of this even possible?

"Captain. We need your orders."

He couldn't do it. If there was even a chance that the phantom *Arkhaven* was real and contained the same cargo as was in the one beneath his feet, he could no more destroy it than he could allow it to destroy him. The timer on the screen ticked ever closer to zero, and the speck of light grew larger and larger as it loomed toward them.

"Prime the Krasnikov Engine."

"But what if—"

Ten seconds.

"Engage it," Sully said.

Five seconds.

The order rippled across the bridge, a warning blared through the vessel and commanded all hands to prepare for an interstellar transit like nothing any human had ever attempted. The *Arkhaven* shuddered as fusion reactors shunted all available energy to the torus in the center of the craft that would tunnel through space time and allow them to attain superluminal speed.

"It's finally happening," Daluxo breathed. "What do you think we'll see as we slip the bonds of time?"

One second. The timer froze. The bulkheads flexed and whined under the strain of the Krasnikov Engine, and the false *Arkhaven* receded.

Sully exhaled. His fingers slipped from where he had clasped them together, sweaty, trembling. The strain of the near collision echoed through his body. He closed his eyes and let his body simply relax. The millions of lives entrusted to his care were safe. Seconds ticked by—seconds that Sully knew were dilated into years outside the boundaries of the Krasnikov tube created by his ship. When he opened his eyes, he wondered how long it had been in real time since their narrow escape.

"What the hell is that?" Daluxo asked. "That's the destination star. It can't have intelligent life. We've spent decades studying it, why would something appear now?"

Sully snapped his eyes to his XO, triggered as much by the gravity implied by they typically proper Daluxo's minor profanity as anything else. Interference from the exotic matter churning in the Krasnikov Engine radiated in chaotic waves and made the ship's sensors dance and scream, but a single stable signature read out amid the noise, unmistakably artificial, and directly in their path.

"And why is it so… recognizably human?" A pit formed in Sully stomach as he opened a radio channel and spoke into the distortion of spacetime that surrounded his ship. "This is the Genesis Ship, *Arkhaven*. Identify yourself, over."

He closed the channel and awaited the reply.

Jonathan Ficke lives outside of Milwaukee with family. See more of his work at jonficke.com or on twitter @jonficke.

Gazing into the Abyss by Ryan Klopp

When the end of the world started, I almost missed it.

I was staring at the chessboard, my brain spinning like a hamster on its wheel, trying to figure out what options I had left. None of them were good, and I looked up for just long enough to see Vanya's half-smile, half-smirk staring back at me. Of course he was winning. The Russki bastard always won, or at least often enough that I could guess the outcome before I ever floated over to the board. Often enough that I suspected the rare times he let me escape with a draw were just to keep me interested.

I rolled over as I began to float away, reaching out to pull myself back into place, grimacing as I lifted a knight and set it back down in front of my king. It was the best move available, but that was very faint praise indeed. All I was doing at this point was delaying the inevitable, but I didn't really mind. Even when you know the end, the journey still matters, or some similarly Zen aphorism about destiny. My wife likes those. I personally tend to go more for pop-culture references, like "there is no fate but what we make." It seemed appropriate when playing chess against the Terminator.

Looking down at the tiny figures spread out between us, I

almost missed the little flash, just a single spot of light in the dark. I frowned and blinked, wondering if I had imagined it. And then the light burned again, a bright flash that, for just an instant, outshone all the others. It came from about halfway up the East Coast, about where Washington should be.

Exactly where Washington should be.

I barely even noticed Vanya floating up beside me, his eyes wider than I'd ever seen them as he stared down at our world. More and more pinpricks of light burst into being, scattered across the entire map. Over and over the cycle repeated, light and then all-consuming darkness, until I couldn't watch any more. For three, four, five seconds, I simply couldn't speak, countless possibilities, explanations, prayers racing themselves through the corridors of my mind. "The radio. There's got to be some kind of transmission, right? Something to tell the world what's going on?"

Without waiting for me, he flipped it to "ON", to the preset Mission Control channel. Nothing. He turned the dials, faster and faster, his breath coming in short gasps.

And then, the sound of a human voice, so quiet I thought for a moment that I had imagined it. A soft, mechanical beep followed by a single sentence. It was in Russian, but that was irrelevant. "*Systema 'Perimeter' aktivirovana.*" "Perimeter system activated."

"That's impossible." Vanya's voice was almost a whisper, then it suddenly, sharply grew into something much louder, into a scream. "What did your people do!?" I knew what the Perimeter system was, every American officer who specialized in Russia did. It was a relic from the Cold War, a relic supposedly dismantled decades ago. A colossal nuclear dead-man switch, an automated system meant as the final defense against a first strike, the USSR's ultimate insurance policy. Even if all of mankind went down with them.

I could see desperation morph into disbelieving rage in his eyes, and I took a deep breath. "My people? What the hell are you talking about, Vanya? My home is the one getting nuked to hell right now, not yours!"

He shook his head from side to side, his face melting into a mask that somehow seemed to be cold, sad, and angry all at once. "We both know what Perimeter is. If it's firing, then I don't have a home anymore."

It suddenly hit me what he was saying, hit me with the force of a truck, and I stared dumbly for a moment. "Or there's a circuit loose somewhere in the machine that hasn't been maintained since the Soviets."

"Maybe." In that instant, he looked so much older than his forty years. He looked like the picture he once showed me of his grandfather, the one who taught him to play chess, the weight of decades bearing down on him. "We're over America now, not Russia. We can't see what's going on there. And it doesn't really matter, does it?" He laughed, a short, mirthless sound. "It's not like you all don't have procedures in place for something like this. Even if there still is a Russia, there won't be by the time we orbit far enough to see it. And then it'll be up to the cockroaches to decide whose fault it was."

***

Vanya was right, as he always was.

An hour later, when we circled over Russia, we could see the fires burning. Neither of us said a word. There was nothing to say.

That was four days ago.

Four days of silently circling a world that was in the process of tearing itself apart, four days of hearing nothing on the radio except that quiet little broadcast that heralded the end of everything, the sins of our ancestors coming back to finish us off. We have enough air and supplies for months, so I suppose Vanya and I are in a pretty good position, all things considered. Maybe some lesser, smarter country will save us someday, maybe a South American or Australian rocket will dock with us and bring us home. Or maybe we'll kill each other before then. I've seen the way Vanya's eyes have started to follow me. I know that, deep down, he blames me for this. Not me personally, but me as an American. I haven't quite reached that state of mind yet, where desperation and fear and anger meld into a sickening cocktail that makes me see my partner for what he is and not who he is. But like I said, we can last for months up here. I've got time.

Ryan Klopp is a full-time student in Williamsburg, Virginia. He specializes in sci-fi, dark fantasy, and horror.

When the Stars Were Wrong by Wendy Nikel

The creature hid in the universe's shadows, and if we'd known that the *Andromeda XI* would cross its path, we'd have avoided that quadrant entirely. Or maybe not. Maybe we did know.

I don't recall.

The log doesn't indicate any intention of approaching the cosmic being, though the man called Tyrol suspects the records aren't entirely accurate. Our other crew member (Vivian, the patch on her suit says) has only rocked and spoken frantic gibberish since the creature enveloped us in its long, curling appendages, fracturing our fragile memories.

Tyrol pores over our records, his stubbly chin jutting out in concentration, madly circling words and phrases he doesn't think he's written. I stand beside him, staring blankly out the window at the being's giant, darting eye. Or at least I assume that's what it is. It's an orb of concentric circles that jerks about, mirroring my movements. Each circle grows incrementally, hypnotically smaller—a Fibonacci sequence tethered to an eyestalk.

"It says we were investigating an asteroid giving off a strange frequency . . . why can't I remember?" Tyrol's pen hovers over the letters, hesitant. He glances at my patch. "Nadia, do you recall how long we've been out here? How far we are from—"

From what? That's the real question, for though some sense of logic or instinct tells us we'd been on a journey to somewhere (or *from* somewhere) neither of us can remember where. Does it even matter, now that our ship is ensnared in some massive being's clutches and our computers are dim and unresponsive?

I don't answer. It's hopeless.

The ship shudders, and instinctively, I reach out to steady myself. A flash of something on my wrist catches my eye, awakens something in me. A memory? A clue? I ease my bulky sleeve back to expose the tattoo.

"PRISONER #7820-02."

Something heavy hits the ship. My heart slams into my rib cage. Prisoner? Of what? And why? What exactly have I forgotten?

"I'll search the storage compartments," I tell Tyrol, and at his look of surprise, I quickly add, "for clues." I'm not ready yet to tell him what I found: not sure what he'd do or if I should trust him. Or if he should trust me.

The longer I search, the stronger my unease and the more persistent the creature's battering upon the hull. There's no escape pod, but that's not all that's missing. The compartments are fake—Medical Supplies and Food, Lab Equipment and Tools—nothing but squares of plastic fused to the ship's walls. If it even is a ship.

The monster's eye stalk follows me, floating from window to window, circling the orb of our prison. I can't shake the sense that it's angry. That it doesn't want me to discover these things. It doesn't want me to remember.

As we stare each another down, its strangely globed eye reflects the red letters of the ship's name from the hull, backward in the reflection but still decipherable: *Andromeda XI.*

The name strikes a chord. Though I still don't know how we got here, I remember the origin of the name, the myth that goes with it. I rush to the window, and there, beyond the eyestalk, is a tether holding us to the asteroid. Trapping us here like the mythological princess awaiting Cetus's wrath. A sacrifice to an angry god.

Ignoring Tyrol's protests, I pry off the control console's cover, but it's empty, bare of wires or circuits. I begin to piece things together. My breath comes fast. Sweat tickles my neck. Apprehension crumbles into panic.

The hull of the ship—no, *prison*—groans with the sound of bending metal. The creature knows that I know. I can feel it worming through my mind, trying to rework the lies and lull me into complacency, again, but I resist, muttering, "Andromeda."

I may not know who sent us here (an enemy? a government? a vengeful alien race?). I may not know if we deserve this. I may not be able to save us from our fate, but I won't sit by and do nothing. The creature's exterior is tough enough to withstand the vacuum of space, but maybe . . . maybe, I can ensure it dies with us, that no more prisoners—no more Andromedas—are sent here again.

"Nadia!" Tyrol reaches out over the sound of Vivian's screams, over the snapping of aluminum bits as I yank panels from the wall, searching for the oxygen tanks and electrical wiring that provide us our limited air and light. The end is coming by tooth or claw or stomach acid, and as I find what I'm searching for, the creature keens and pushes us inside, enveloping us in utter darkness as the walls crumple around me.

My mind splinters. Plots, strategies, plans die half-realized, lost between broken synapses, disappearing like the stars. I grasp at my fragmented ideas, fumbling for meaning. *Andromeda.* It's the small things that I can cling to.

The ink on Tyrol's wrist, matching my own.

The pink, fleshy throat tissue, contracting outside the cracking glass of a window.

The valve on the oxygen tank, open and leaking.

The wires connecting, igniting a spark.

And my final thought as the universe bursts wide open: the ship's name on my patch.

Andromeda, taking her revenge.

Wendy Nikel is a speculative fiction author with a degree in elementary education, a fondness for road trips, and a terrible habit of forgetting where she's left her cup of tea. Her short fiction has been published by *Fantastic Stories of the Imagination, Daily Science Fiction, Nature: Futures,* and elsewhere. Her time travel novella, *The Continuum,* was published by World Weaver Press in January 2018, with a sequel following in July. For more info, visit wendynikel.com

His Anchor Chains Will Never Break
by Markus Wessel

The gelato is particularly creamy today. Santino stands at the counter of Sweetums Cool Delights and drags his scoop across the chocolate cream, shaping it to resemble waves at high sea. The smell of sugar, vanilla, cocoa, and other spices fills the air, heavy and thick. He is surprised that the perfume of the soldier in front of him cuts through it. Lavender.

She is tall, taller than him, and wears a uniform with the silver eagle of the Interplanetary Security Forces on her shoulder pads with corporal bars beneath. He used to wear a uniform himself, but with different insignia. Long ago, though. Long, but not long enough.

A flash: Skulls smashed like crushed egg-boxes, laser-burns, black streaks on bleached bone...

Santino bites down hard. Not now, please, not again. Put it away. Put it away and close the door. He swallows hard and tastes bile. Still, he drags his face into a smile for the customer. "Good day to you, Corporal. Which might it be? Everything is all-natural here, nothing is artificial."

"I heard." If she recognizes his accent, she doesn't mention it. She squints at the selection behind the glass. "Which one do you like best?"

Sweat wets his flanks below the candystriped cotton shirt. "They are all excellent choices, perfect specimen of Italian artisanship from old Earth. I suggest you try almond. Care for a taste?" Please go, please go, please turn around and go!

She nods and Santino drags a plastic spoon through the ochre gelato, leaving a furrow like a trench.

Flames fill a tunnel and soldiers become running torches, soldiers in uniforms like hers. One reaches out to Santino with eyes melting down his face like boiling jelly. Screams vibrate his bones. He fires again.

"Is everything all right?" She looks at him, *her* eyes large and green.

Santino's heart races, but he catches himself, nods. "It's nothing. Please." His hand shakes as he offers her the spoon.

"That's really good." She moans. "I'll have two scoops, please."

"Of course." Santino stacks two balls the size of childrens' fists on a chocolate-rimmed waffle cone. "There you go. Enjoy." His whole body itches, the scar tracing down the side of his leg a white-hot wire on his skin. He feels his fist clench and he pushes it deep into his pocket, the fingernails digging painfully into the flesh of his palm.

"Thank you," she says as she swipes her wristpad over the register. A green light, the sound of bells, she has paid.

Warships descend from the clouds over the capital, skirting the searchlights that reach for them like white fingers. Others stay high and release bombs that sail down almost in slow-motion and flood the streets with blinding fire. Reports come in, their ground troops are close. It's the last day of the war and Santino crouches in a drain ditch, praying for it to end.

He only stops shaking well after the soldier has left.

Good. He grips the counter with both hands like a helmsman in a storm. Good. The memories breach the fortifications of his mind like an invading force. He smells the blood and the steel and the smoke, hears the sirens, watches the melting carriers spill burning units into the night, watches them fall seconds later. He is there, but isn't. Hasn't been for years. He fights to stay, though, to feel the pain, to take it all in, to let it char and blacken and cauterize his soul. To finally break him into pieces and wrench his mind from its anchor chains. Because he needs it. Because he deserves it. Because he remembers. Because he remembers what he did, and that it can never be forgotten. And he submits.

Markus Wessel is a genre writer from Germany. He lives in an ancient city on the River Rhine and marvels at how deeply memory and place are often interlinked.

Iron and Ice by Matt Bliss

The metallic clang of the lieutenant's rifle tapping against the access hatch rang out in sharp bursts over the frozen wasteland. A riveted steel tube stuck out of the surrounding ice and snow like a monolith; the only vertical thing in the vast whiteness other than the soldiers huddled around it.

With a raised hand, the lieutenant pointed two fingers at the hatch. One of his men slung his rifle, then twisted the handle. Despite its frozen and ancient appearance, the wheel spun with the ease of greased bearings, retracting the bolts that locked it with a resounding click.

They descended a ladder to a corrugated floor. Cold monitors and screens lined the wall, dim as the barren land outside.

"What is this place?" asked the sergeant as his light scanned the space.

"That's what we're going to find out. Keep moving." He motioned to the tunnel opening at the end of the room.

Other than recent satellite images, nothing was known about the mysterious facility. Polar ice melt was doing more than raise sea levels, increase coastal erosion, and cause massive storm surges—it unearthed things lying dormant under layers of ice. Metallic openings. Doors to underground facilities. This concerned politicians more than their own climate change, so they sent one team to investigate.

In a flurry of boots and well-practiced movements, they followed the tunnel deeper under the ice and further into the compound.

As they spread into the next room, their lights fixed on a single object.

"We have something," said the front-man. "A body."

He kept his rifle pointed at the pale corpse on the chair. Its small neck was split open, exposing bone and tendon in a mess of frozen blood. Blood that looked black in their beam of light.

"What the hell is—"

"Get a sample," snapped the lieutenant.

The men stared at the small body's sharp features and bulbous eyes—frozen in a blank upward stare. It lay sprawled over a console of buttons and gauges, each marked with unreadable symbols.

"Russian? Chinese?" said one of the men, pointing to the markings.

The lieutenant shook his head. "No. I don't know what this is..."

A steel pounding echoed from further in the facility. The team raised their rifles to the entryway as puffs of white breath blocked their line of sight. In a series of hand signals, they moved into formation and pressed forward into the tunnels.

Their rifles followed pipes and wires tracing the walls of the shaft until widening into a hall. A hall lined with a series of large upright tubes. Each man breathed the frigid air in fast, shallow breaths at the sight.

Someone wiped a gloved hand over the nearest, freeing the frost clinging to it before staggering back. A small motionless creature, similar to the one they found, stared back through round bulging eyes. He watched as a bubble escaped its sliver of a mouth to rise through the viscous green fluid surrounding it.

"Boss..." he reached an arm for the man, refusing to tear his eyes away. "These... things... what—"

"I don't know." The lieutenant scanned his light over its pointed features.

The men jerked back to the tunnel opening as pounding echoed from inside. Each bang sent a blast of cooled air with it, and each blast filled them with an icy dread. The men pointed their rifles at the dark opening, waiting for the order.

With a waved hand, the team filed into the next room, weapons raised. Their aim flicked from one target to the next. Scanning over multiple bodies that lay scattered across the dark clearing. Each one similar to the creatures they found earlier. Each one mangled and twisted in a violent end.

Movement from the corner drew them away from the terror. A pale creature stumbled forward, hand to its neck as blood dripped from between its small fingers. Its globelike eyes squinted at the lights beaming from the team.

It sputtered and coughed before it fell to the floor, and the soldiers moved to its side.

"What happened here?" one asked, crouching beside the growing red puddle. "Can you speak?"

Its eyes glittered through the darkness as if fire burned on the other side. The group watched the flame dim. It raised a shaking finger to the darkened doorway from which he came, and gurgled words that sent a shiver down each of their spines.

"He's coming..." it said through choking coughs before eventually lying still. The fire was gone.

The team raised their rifles to see a large hulking form move toward them, shaking the floor with each massive step. It stopped only paces away, pointing the barrel of a weapon at the soldiers who stood frozen in disbelief.

"You've all been very naughty this last year," it said in a gravel-laden voice, "and it's time that I put an end to it." He racked the slide of the weapon and grinned below rosy cheeks. He pulled the trigger and let out a unique laugh as screams and gunshots echoed through the facility.

Matt Bliss drinks too much coffee and writes speculative fiction in Las Vegas, Nevada. Find him on Twitter at @MattJBliss.

The Final Voyage by Dorian J. Sinnott

This wasn't the first time Captain Greene had been on a mission. He was seasoned in his career, venturing across the vastness of space. Well earning the title he carried. It was, however, the first time he had been sent alone. Alone, that is, as the sole sentient being. The only human.

Unlike Greene, this was his crewmates' first flight. Their first mission outside the secured testing facilities. A final test of their ability to adapt to true space. Atmospheres beyond the Earth's surface. They were a pricey investment, but one the government had been adamant on implementing. One that would save millions years down the road. Reduce the need for human production. A fully robotic exploration crew to search the universe—to go places that mankind could never set foot. Robonauts. That's what they called them. An android suit—void of any life within it. Just wires and microchips. The solution to the future of space exploration. And protection.

* * *

Greene ran his fingers through his hair as he logged the last of the day's report. There were no changes, nothing spotted out amongst the stars. He knew they would soon be approaching

Mars for exploration. The final task to test the Robonauts and their ability to function and thrive outside of the shuttle.

There were no dangers so far, he documented. No encounters of life amidst the galaxy. No threats to the shuttle as it continued towards the red planet—just beyond the stars.

And Greene was thankful for that.

The crew before him weren't as lucky. Their craft had been blown off course by a meteor shower, sending them to planetary depths they hadn't been prepared for. Climate-wise. Lifeform-wise.

None of them made it back alive.

The sounds of their screams and pleas to the space station still gripped his memory. Ate away at his mind. They hadn't been prepared, he told himself. But, at least, he was. He kept his gun close by, out of fear something would emerge. Crawl out from the deep, darkness surrounding him. But he had been lucky. He kept telling himself that.

This was the last mission. And then he could retire from the stars. Retire from the many months away from Earth. These would be the Robonauts' missions now. Their concern.

And no more lives would be lost. At least, not human.

That, to Greene, was the most valuable part of this final voyage.

* * *

In the late hours, however, Greene was awoken. Shaken from his sleep by the rattling shuttle. Its once smooth course was rickety, rocking back and forth. Hitting a rough patch of turbulence. Heavy space winds cycloning through the skies.

The very winds he feared. The ones that deterred the crew

before him.

Greene hurried to the cockpit, struggling to get the craft back on a steady track. Outside, beams of light streaked through the darkness. Shooting like stars. Cosmic rays of gas and flame. He did all he could to steer the shuttle out of the path of the falling debris. Away from impact.

The only choice he had was the quickly approaching surface of Mars. Bracing himself, he allowed the craft to touch down, colliding heavily with the ground beneath.

The lights flashed within the shuttle as it struck the surface, warning systems blaring as Greene shut his eyes. It all happened at once. Flashes of red and white. Alarms. Emergency alerts. Cabin pressure failing. But then, all was silent. Dark.

The systems shut down. And the lights in the sky stopped falling.

Now, there was nothing but darkness. Waiting for the sun to rise.

* * *

Greene scoped the cabin with what little light he was able to from his flashlight. His attempts to radio the base and report the incident failed. Just as he expected. With a heavy sigh, he made his way through the craft, inspecting any damage he may have found. Damage he was certain of.

He prayed that the storm had merely knocked out the system and not the impact itself. Something that could be rebooted. Hours of waiting, but at least a fixable repair. One that would allow him to complete his mission and return home. Safely. In one piece.

As he rounded the corner towards the breaker room, he was

unaware of the shifting in the shadows. The red glowing lights beneath helmets. The Robonauts. Awoken.

* * *

The beam of the flashlight was shaky as Greene tripped the switches, listening to the shuttle breathe back to life. The power surged, releasing a deep roar as it moved from the back of the craft to the front. It would be a while before everything was up and running, Greene knew that. But his first thoughts were on the radio. If he could get to that... Send a signal. Report in. At least then he would have contact. Hope.

As he turned to head back towards the main cabin, he was stopped by a figure in the doorway. It towered over him, in a full flight suit and helmet. Practically human in every way—except the red, glowing eyes.

"I guess the Robonauts were the first to reboot," Greene said, clearing his throat.

The machine in the doorway's head twitched. From behind it, Greene could see more of them, making their way down the hall. Eyes burning deep red. It took only a moment for him to feel the twinge in his chest at the realization. The fear seeping in. Noticing his gun, the one he had left in the cockpit, in the Robonaut's hand. Slowly rising towards his temple.

The reboot.

The Robonauts, built for exploration and protection—a high tech intergalactic military—had a change of mission. Rewritten by the falling stars. The system waves. The space winds. They were no longer there to protect, but destroy. Their final test, beyond the Earth's surface. In the loneliness of space.

As the hot tears streamed down Greene's face, he couldn't

help but smile. Whether failed or succeeded, his mission had been fulfilled.

Dorian J. Sinnott's word has appeared in over 200 journals and has been nominated for the Best of the Net. Find him on Twitter @doriansinnott

Used Armor Smell by A. P. Howell

Janot's armor no longer had that new-armor smell.

New-armor smell was different from new-suit smell; was different from new-car smell and new-carpet smell. But all of those scents pinged something in the human brain, created a sense of purity. Said *this* was a new thing, recently created by complex industrial processes, but untouched by human hands. (Except technicians and installers and salespeople and logistics specialists and—it was always rumored, no matter what the usage hours buried in HUD settings claimed—an unlucky previous owner who'd hemorrhaged all over the interior.) The newness smelled of ownership, mastery, and exclusive rights.

The new-armor smell had faded, replaced by Janot's own smell. Usually, it was undetectable. The armor did an excellent job of wicking away sweat and cycling the air (it still smelled like recycled air, but Janot couldn't recall the last time e'd inhaled unmediated atmosphere). The armor's plumbing was mated to Janot's—no diapers, no drips, no offensive odors—and sometimes e missed the catheter while walking down a corridor to the toilet.

The armor was even good about cleaning vomit. Janot could smell it, however, and there were still bits splattered on eir faceplate, visible behind the urgent reds of the HUD. E could also smell the coppery scent of blood.

Couldn't feel the arm at all, not since the whiteout pain of…seconds earlier? When shit happened, it happened fast. The HUD reported painkillers and stimulants and tourniquet protocols: bright bullet points that could be easily dismissed, distractions from survival. Janot tried to flex eir fingers and the gauntlet flexed in response.

Did e even *have* those fingers any more, or was the gauntlet just filled with red jelly, reacting to nervous impulses sent to a limb that no longer existed?

Beyond the HUD, beyond the faceplate, the world was dark and full of smoke and fire. Weapons fire, bright traceries crossing the sky to their terminus, and the orange-red evidence of atmospheric O2. Janot could only see eir unit with the HUD, and it showed fewer points of light than e liked. The enemy was completely invisible.

The armor's systems gave Janot an instant's warning before the igneous rock formation at eir back split and exploded outward. Time enough to lunge away, flattened to the ground. The new wave of red warnings indicated blunt force impacts, nothing to compromise the armor.

Janot tried to move. The arm e could feel and the arm e couldn't both moved, no sign of exacerbated injury. One leg fine, one pinned under a hunk of rock that had melted along some of its surfaces and was hot enough there to do some minor damage to the armor. The angle was awkward but e rose to eir knees, arms and back pushing against the weight on eir calf and foot. It shifted—Janot felt it in the changing angle and saw it in the HUD, couldn't feel it in the leg; it had either been protected by the armor or the pain masked by the meds. Janot wanted to check, but navigating the HUD's menus seemed too complex a task.

Not a good sign. The sounds echoing in eir ears—not quite ringing, not quite a whine—clearly originated in Janot's own skull.

Also a bad sign.

E was on eir feet, rifle grasped in both gauntlets, moving toward a highlighted position on the HUD's map. Not a decision Janot had made, not a movement e had made. E cycled through readouts, almost at random, saw the spike in the armor's processing. It was running very expensive calculations. The situational awareness built over the course of human evolution was difficult to replicate computationally, even with the expert training dumped into expert systems.

A painfully bright point lit up the HUD. The rifle snapped up. Janot registered the recoil, deadened by the armor, and then the disappearance of the bright point. E looked past the display, a reflex despite knowing the target wouldn't be visible. Oily black smoke boiled in the air, but Janot's attention was caught by the red speckling on the inside of the faceplate. Eir next exhalation added more.

E moved through the smoke, rifle ready to engage. That processing flare was back and growing stronger, the armor making decisions Janot couldn't. (Wouldn't? But no, the armor was doing what it was supposed to do—what e was supposed to do—moving toward the objective glowing on the map.)

E tried to feel the good arm, the good leg, the pinned leg, finally whatever was left of the bad arm. The way the skinsuit snagged against the armor when e lifted a leg, the pressure just above the knee, the place e tapped eir thumbnail against the gauntlet...nothing. Janot dug through menus in search of medical readouts. Was the system burying them so e wouldn't be distracted? Not that it mattered. E couldn't get a medevac in the middle of a firefight. The system was doing what it could, the processing graph burning into Janot's retinas.

Another flare on the map and the armor took the shot. This time, something returned fire and pressure blossomed across Janot's ribs. The armor took a second shot and the enemy disappeared from the HUD.

Janot could barely see that detail. The world beyond the faceplate blurred—some of that seemed like motion, the armor bearing em implacably forward, but Janot couldn't tell for sure, eir sense of balance perhaps damaged with eir hearing. E tried to say something, even though there was no one to listen. E tasted more blood.

Janot couldn't smell recycled air any more, or even vomit, only the smell of blood. The smell of emself, of desperation and hopelessness.

A. P. Howell writes science fiction, fantasy, and horror. She can be found online at aphowell.com or on Twitter @APHowell.

Sensitive Matters by Grant Butler

I remember the day it happened. It was November 1961, just days after the annual Revolution Day celebration in Red Square. A call just before dawn summoned me to a top-secret military base to handle what I was told was a rocket test that had experienced difficulties.

The first thing that comes to mind about that morning was that it was bitingly cold. The chill was thick even inside the base. But I didn't complain. None of us did. We were part of an elite group of officers within the Soviet Union specially trained to handle "sensitive matters."

Despite the obvious differences from America, we had our own version of what is referred to as Area 51. But there was never so much open speculation and public interest about what existed in the Soviet Union. We didn't speculate about some remote speck of land in the Nevada desert because we had the entire country to speculate over.

"Good morning, Comrade Volkov." The general in charge of the facility greeted me with a crisp salute that made his medals jingle. "It has been requested that we oversee the recovery of a rocket test that failed to succeed."

"Of course, Comrade General." I nodded before myself and the others were escorted to a convoy of military vehicles that took us out to a dense forest. I'd been on numerous assignments like it as part of the group overseeing "sensitive matters."

The journey was long, cold, and everywhere we went there were plenty of people in both uniform and casual attire keeping watch on the roads. The sky was still pitch dark and was beautiful to look at. The night sky never fails to remind me that in the vastness of space, Earth is nothing more than a tiny apartment in a skyscraper that seems limitless.

The convoy finally stopped, and we all set out on foot towards a dense cluster of pines. About a mile into the trees there was a twisted mass of steel and other metals smoldering on the grass. From the fallen trees, it was clear whatever it was had crashed and landed here. The wreckage looked like it was smoldering, but the heat coming off it was mild. Like that from the many outdoor fires I had spent many a night in front of while on watch somewhere during the war. I had never seen anything like it, and it didn't look like any rocket I'd seen before. And I'd seen plenty.

Men in various uniforms surrounded the gnarled cluster of metal. Some were outfitted for a chemical incident, others held special radiation equipment, while others simply stood around with a lit cigarette. None of them looked quite sure of what to do.

"Results?" The General in charge turned to one of the people with radiation equipment.

"Clear." The man answered back.

The General nodded. "Alright. Our orders are to escort it to the mountain facility, where further tests and research will be conducted."

He stepped aside and a massive military truck pulled up in front of the wreckage. The back was swiftly unloaded, and a battalion of men stepped out. Once they pulled on thick gloves, they joined the others, and a captain began ordering them how to lift and load the wreckage into the truck. The air was filled with grunts before the object was lifted into the air and carefully carried to the truck. I could tell from the look on their faces that whatever the wreckage was, it was surprisingly light to carry. Far lighter than it looked.

They carefully eased it up into the truck and slammed the hatch before they piled into another truck that was waiting nearby. But just before the hatch was closed, I saw a flicker of movement within the wreckage. It was subtle, barely noticeable if you weren't paying close attention, but it was there.

I carefully glanced around to see if anyone else had noticed. If they had, they gave no sign of it. That was no surprise. So I did the same thing and acted like I hadn't seen it. Not that it was easy, as the sight sent a shiver through my body that I pretended was just a chill from the cold.

"Well done gentleman." The General nodded around before he started walking back towards our vehicles. That was the cue to follow him.

I never figured out what the wreckage was, if anything was in it, or what was done with it. Although I suspect it's still here somewhere, carefully hidden away. The past doesn't fade away easily. It's always just waiting to be rediscovered.

Grant Butler is the author of the novel The Heroin Heiress and his short fiction has been published in Sick Cruising and Mardi Gras Mysteries.

Wax Soldiers by Kurt Newton

The landscape was a maze of abandoned buildings and cobble-stone alleyways. Heaps of rubble forced Simms to navigate through a crumbling tenement in the hope of reaching his checkpoint. He had become separated from his unit, but it wasn't the first time he had found himself in enemy territory outnumbered and outgunned.

Simms climbed through a blast hole in the building's south wall and stepped into another narrow alleyway. The alley brought him to the edge of a courtyard. He stopped to listen for the march of foot soldiers, and was about to break into the open when he heard a tumble of brick from behind. He wheeled, gun raised. It was one of *them*—tall, thin, dressed in black body armor, black boots, black faceplate. The plate was contoured to mimic human features, yet designed to render them featureless, uniform, indistinguishable from each other.

Simms shot, his reflexes responding to the sudden threat. The soldier landed in a sitting position against the rubble, the bullet piercing the combatant's forehead. Simms walked over and lifted the shield. The face beneath was just as featureless. As Simms examined the soldier for intel, the head wound began to close. Soon, there would be nothing of the wound but a small circular blemish. Simms didn't wait around. The gun-shot had drawn attention.

He scrambled out into the open and ducked behind a debris pile: the remains of what was once a church. A stone cross jutted from the pile like the mast of a sunken ship. Pieces of stained glass littered the ground.

Three soldiers marched into view.

Simms checked his gun clip. Only one round left. It could have been a hundred for all it mattered. He had shot at them before. The bullets tugged at their uniform but they just kept coming.

Simms surveyed his surroundings. There was an abandoned truck ten yards away, its engine compartment destroyed by a grenade, however its gas tank appeared intact. Simms hoped this to be so. It was his last chance. He waited for the soldiers to pass near the truck, took aim and fired.

The truck lifted off the ground, exploding in a fireball. The soldiers lay lifeless beneath a rain of shrapnel. Simms should have run, but instead he approached the burning wreck and the bodies that lay beside it. Each of the soldiers had been burned by the blast—uniform charred and smoldering, face gone, wiped clean by the flames.

Simms worked quickly, collecting weapons and ammo. When the heat became unbearable, he stepped back, but it wasn't soon enough. His hand began to drip, the skin sloughing off. He stepped back further and the dripping slowed, then stopped altogether. Almost immediately, the damaged skin began to regenerate, filling in the portions he had lost.

By now, the enemy soldiers were nearly unrecognizable as men, just clothing resting atop puddles of liquid slag. But Simms knew, once the truck had burned itself out, they too would return to what they were. It was the way of war; it was never-ending.

Simms looked toward the sky to check the position of the sun. He then chose a direction and fled before more soldiers arrived.

Simms reached his checkpoint by sundown rejuvenated, ready for the next battle.

Kurt Newton's flash fiction has appeared in Daily Science Fiction, Black Infinity and The Arcanist.

Snows Of Years Gone by Robert Dawson

Larisse sits among the hibernacula and plucks an angular melody from the strings of her chitarre. The bare concrete walls give the cryostasis room the acoustics of a concert hall. The tune is four hundred years old, the words a thousand.

"Dictes moy ou, n'en quel pays" she sings,
"Est Flora, la belle Romaine…"

Tell me where, in what land, is Flora, the Roman beauty? asked Francois Villon in medieval Paris. Where are Heloise, Beatrice, Blanche de Castille? It's two in the morning, there's nobody else on the night shift to hear; and Larisse sings Villon's words for the woman who lies, frozen a few degrees above absolute zero, in the pod beside her. And you, Nina my love, where are you? she thinks, as her lips continue the song. Your body is right here, but where have *you* gone?

"Et Jehanne, la bonne Lorraine
Qu'Anglois bruslerent a Rouen…"

The verse ends. Larisse falls silent, lets the last chord die away. Like Joan of Arc, burned by the English in Rouen, Nina had fought the extraterrestrial invaders with every fierce fiber of her being. She had come home safe from the Battle of Japan, all brash grin and crewcut. She'd survived Antarctica with only mild radiation poisoning. But she'd been flown home from the Second European Action in a medically-induced coma, her lithe body so broken that the medics had offered no hope short of cryogenic stasis. Five years, they said, ten at the outside; nanotechnology improves every year, and soon we'll be able to heal her. Weeping, Larisse signed the papers; and they froze sweet Nina, and placed her in one of the cryostasis centers that were sprouting like mushrooms.

Weeks later, a bomb–Earth's, the enemy's, who knew?—destroyed the university where Larisse taught. The next day she packed her things, got on a train, and talked her way into a job as a guard here, where Nina waits to be healed. Outside, Earth's devastated economy struggles to recover; wages are low, food is scarce, and electrical power unreliable. But Nina and her comrades await their day of return like King Arthur's knights in Avalon, their pods powered by a near-immortal micronuke generator in the basement.

There is a noise out in the hall, feet, nervous voices. *Intruders.* Larisse silently lays her chitarre on the floor and takes up a wicked-looking laser gun. Slowly, she turns, aims the gun toward the door, and stands motionless.

Soon four people—three men and a woman, all stunted by malnourishment, probably none over twenty-five—tiptoe into the crypt. They carry crowbars and hacksaws: looters, after copper and steel. They've got nothing powerful enough to break through the heavy outer doors: somebody must have sold them the passcode. They haven't noticed her yet.

"You!" she shouts. "Halt!" They startle, turn; a crowbar clangs to the floor. One kid reaches for a weapon: she burns him down. He shrieks, but only for a moment; the others drop their tools and run for their lives. Larisse lets them go, takes a shaky breath, then walks over and makes sure that the kid's dead. She has few regrets: there is nothing in this building to steal except parts of the machinery that keeps Nina and the others frozen. For an armload of metal, this pathetic scavenger would have let them thaw and rot. She kicks the skinny corpse viciously, hears a rib crack, then grabs an arm and drags the body out of the podroom, down the corridor, and out through the gaping door into the night. More gently, her anger and frustration ebbing, she pushes the body against the wall and leaves it for the coyotes and the crows. She goes back inside, clangs the door shut and, tongue pressed against teeth, makes an emergency change in the passcode. The supervisor can set up a proper one in the morning.

And this is what we've has come to, she thinks, in the thirty years since we defeated the invaders. A world of beggars, fighting over crusts. One day, perhaps, there will be money for food, for education, for that long-promised nanotechnology research. Until then, Nina and her comrades must sleep.

She walks back to the cryopod, and picks up the chitarre.

"Prince, n'enquerez de sepmaine
 Ou elles sont, ne de cest an,
 Qu'a ce refrain ne vous remaine:
 Mais ou sont les neiges d'antan?"

Tell me, Nina, my love: where, where are the snows of years

gone by?

Robert Dawson's fiction has appeared in numerous anthologies and periodicals. He believes the world needs more bicycles.

X-21 by Joe Scipione

I couldn't see anything. The planet was dark and when the tech went down, there was no light at all. Our helmets were off and our eyes hadn't adjusted to the dark. I didn't know if they ever would. Even the plasma rifle was off. Thankfully, I had grandpa's old pistol as a backup. I pulled it out.

"Foster, what do you see?" My partner, Cole, called from somewhere in the darkness.

"Not much," I called to her. "I can barely see my hand in front of my face."

There was movement and Cole slid down next to me, I could just make out her face in the darkness.

"You think they're all dead?" She asked. The rest of our team had been a few hundred meters ahead of us. Something black and amorphous appeared, it enveloped them seconds before the world went dark.

"I don't know. They just...disappeared." I felt crazy saying it but that was how it went down. The advance team was in front of us, scouting the forest on this planet. We'd been assured it was safe. Every inch of the planet had been scanned—fifty meters deep—it was classified UNINHABITED and we were the first on-site team. This was the 21st planet—we'd never encountered a problem. Until today.

I leaned back against the nearest tree. The tree was massive—five times wider than me, as tall as most skyscrapers on earth. My hands shook, we needed to get the situation under control.

"Alright," I said. "We're stuck here for now. Martinez and the Doc are back on the ship but they aren't able to talk to us. They'll scan for life signs and come down to pick us up once they see the rest of the team is gone."

"Right," Cole said. "Once Martinez sees two life signs, he'll come down in the rover."

I nodded.

"As long as that thing doesn't come back, we should be okay. There's not supposed to be *anything* on this planet," Cole continued her thought.

We went silent, listening to the strange sounds of the planet. Every planet sounds different. It was not something I was prepared for but exploring twenty new planets in five years taught me pretty fast. Silence on one planet was different from silence on another. I'd signed up to explore—same as Cole. We'd trained to protect ourselves but we were geologists—not soldiers. The others were there for protection, we were there for science. But, with that thing lurking out there, we were about to become soldiers and fight for our lives. It was unspoken between us. For that reason, we let the silence of this planet hang in the air.

"Tasha," Cole said. "Are you ready for this? We're going to have to fight to live through this, I think."

"I'm ready." I said. "I've got grandpa's pistol ready to go. You guys all laughed at me when I loaded out with it. Now look at me."

"Yeah," I could hear the smile in Cole's voice. "I guess you're right. All I got is this damn knife."

"Well, let's hope we don't have to use either one," I said.

"Let's hope."

The words weren't even out of her mouth when the silence of the planet was replaced by a different sound. It was unlike anything I'd heard before—on this planet or any other. Something moved toward us through the darkness. I prayed for a light, for the power to return in our suits or Martinez to get his ass to the surface and pick us up. But I got none of those things. Instead, it was whatever had swallowed the rest of our team.

"Hear that?" Cole said.

"Yep," I drew the old pistol, flipped off the safety.

The sound was louder, closer. It was next to us. Above us. All around us.

I lifted the pistol to the black, amorphous shape. I could feel it in every direction expanding and contracting—like it was breathing. I leveled the gun and squeezed down on the trigger; certain the resulting explosion would make the thing swallow us like it had done to our friends.

The gun fired.

It worked. The thing was gone. The silence of the planet returned.

I opened my mouth to celebrate but was drowned out by another sound. This one was the familiar sound of the rover coming in for a landing, the light on its front illuminating our surroundings. I'd never been so happy to see Martinez through cockpit window. He gave a thumbs up, then his eyes widened; his face, one of shock. We turned.

"Tasha, run!" Cole shouted. I was already grabbing her arm, pulling her toward the rover.

The light from the rover shone on the inky mass. It grew and shrunk, floating a few meters off the ground. It darted at us as we ran. I knew we couldn't out run it and turned to fire the pistol again. Next to me, Cole tripped and fell to the ground, she reached for me to stop her fall, knocking the gun from my hand. Cole and the pistol slid to the ground. I tried to pull her up but she scrambled and reached for the gun.

"Run!" She grabbed the gun and turned to face the thing. I was two steps closer to the rover but stopped to watch. I should have grabbed her then, but I didn't. She fired. The thing didn't stop this time. Black ink surrounded her. She was gone. I screamed and it turned toward me. I ran and dove for the open hatch of the rover. Martinez pulled up and away just as the thing went for me. It couldn't move as fast as the rover and we managed to get away.

We radioed home and marked the planet now known as X-21 as INHABITED and off-limits to future exploration.

Joe Scipione is the author of Perhaps She Will Die and Zoo: Eight Tales of Animal Horror.

Inside the Wire by Zachary Whalen

"This your first night watch, kid?"

Mannix swung around, squinting through a flashlight's beam at the marine standing behind her. The light switched off with a click and she saw him better under the floodlights: tall, broad-shouldered and with no helmet on his tight black curls. He wore a relaxed grin and a rifle slung over one shoulder.

"That obvious?" Mannix asked him.

The dark haired man stepped closer and gently pushed the barrel of Mannix's rifle away from his chest. From this distance, she could read the name embroidered on his gray fatigues — Cabot.

"You're squeezing that thing like it's fixin' to jump out of your hands," he drawled. "Come on, take five."

Cabot leaned his rifle against a railing on the catwalk where they overlooked the Forward Operating Base's single gate and its outer checkpoint. He turned his back on the drab tents and pre-fab sheds of the compound below to gaze out through the loops of barbed wire atop the base's concrete fence.

Mannix looked around for the night watch captain but he was nowhere to be seen. She set her rifle down beside Cabot's then leaned on the fence, letting her eyes follow the checkpoint's dirt road until it vanished in the craggy desert beyond the reach of the floodlights.

The distant ridges that surrounded the base were only jagged shadows now, set against the dark purple of the night sky. Above them, the crescents of two opalescent moons gleamed among unfamiliar stars. For the first time since her arrival on the planet, Mannix was struck by Calyce's beauty. The whine of the checkpoint's unmanned turret pivoting on its tripod broke the desert's peaceful silence.

"They sent a lot of firepower just to guard some driller bots on a barren planet," Mannix said. Cabot scoffed in answer.

"You really are new here, huh?"

"Just rotated in yesterday."

"Me, I'm on my way out." Cabot took a pack of menthols from his breast pocket and offered her one. She pulled out and sparked her lighter, shielding its flame from the chilling breeze as she lit both their cigarettes. "Back to Homer, Louisiana," Cabot went on. "Ever been down there?" Mannix shook her head.

"What did you mean, when I brought up the turret?"

Cabot regarded her as he took a drag. "Did you look up this place before you shipped out?" he asked.

Mannix shrugged. "Dead rock, lots of ore, no intelligent life before or since they parked the mining outpost here." Cabot grinned and wagged a finger at her.

"Or so they say. You ever check the deployment rosters? Interesting reads. You'll notice that a lot of marines go missing despite having nothing to do but stand guard and count rocks."

Mannix looked warily at the crater-pocked desert stretching away from the checkpoint. "You're telling me there's something out there?" she asked. "Why wouldn't they brief us about it?

What's the point of pretending we're alone here?"

"It's because of the locals and their juju," Cabot told her.

Mannix's puzzled stare was her only reply.

"They're crafty types," he explained. "Between their anatomy and static from the native geology nothing catches 'em on the move. Scanners, sensors, the recon drones... it's all junk here. Us proud grunts are the last line of defence, and the brass think ignorance keeps us safe."

Mannix realized she had been gawking when the cigarette burnt her fingers. She flicked the ash off and asked Cabot, "Keep us safe from what?"

"The juju," he repeated solemnly. "The locals make you see things that aren't there — jump at shadows. Before you realize it, it's too late. And the more afraid you are, the easier it is to play their tricks on you."

"Shit..."

Mannix took a long drag, mulling over what Cabot had told her and how it explained the dread that had been gnawing at her stomach since her platoon arrived planetside the night before.

A whir from the sweeping turret caught her attention in the stillness. She peered down through the coils of wire and the checkpoint booth's plastic windows. The jaundiced yellow light within fell on an empty desk and a blank monitor. No one there — not that she could see, anyway — and although she leaned forward until her helmet brushed the wire there was no sign of anyone on guard below, either.

"You really don't remember Cabot, do you?" he asked with feigned offense. Mannix turned and saw him flashing his pearly white smile again.

"Remember you... from where?"

"Basic." Cabot chuckled and stubbed out his cigarette. "He

washed out after a week. 'Lacked discipline,' they said. Stuck around just long enough for you to remember his cute smile and the name of that backwater town he came from."

Mannix's heart was already racing before the words sunk in. She studied Cabot's grinning face, finally placing it from boot camp. The smile was just right, but his eyes were colder now. She glanced at the rifles leaning beside them.

"Oh, I warned you. It's too late now." Cabot — she could still only bring herself to think of it as Cabot — was staring at her with an almost apologetic expression. "They let you down from the start — your officers. They hid us from you, trying to protect you from fear. But when a guard is patrolling at night, with a gun, wondering what they could possibly be searching the darkness of an empty desert for, the fear has already set in."

Cabot flicked his cigarette away and it vanished into thin air. Mannix looked down at hers and saw only her empty hands spread before her.

There was a sharp pain at her back, then numbness and two jutting pincers slick with blood protruding through her chest.

"It was nice talking with you, Sharon," Cabot's voice echoed in her mind. "But it's time for me to meet your friends."

Zachary Whalen writes audio description scripts by day and fiction by night. Follow him on Twitter @SuperWhalen.

Princess of Ruin by Heather Santo

Ellis moved his mop along the floor. He was in Storage Room 7, sweating in a thick, uncomfortable biohazard suit. Inset LED bulbs in the ceiling emitted a soft, white glow, and steel walls surrounded him on all four sides. Once a month, Ellis sterilized the walls using a portable steam vapor disinfectant system. Although tedious, he completed this task efficiently and without complaint. Stable employment, even janitorial work, was hard to come by.

Especially for an uneducated war orphan.

He considered himself lucky. The job, despite low pay, included an efficiency apartment on the outskirts of the compound, as well two meals as day. When applying, Ellis discovered only candidates with no living relatives would be considered. "A containment safeguard, in the unlikely event of a health breach," explained a mountainous, obviously ex-military man during the interview process.

"My family died in the West Coast fire bombings," Ellis replied. His parents were lucky, too. They'd died before the bio attacks.

Now, his heavy breathing filled the suit hood, drowning the steady hum of rows of cryogenic chambers. Inside each glass and metal box, a person lay face up, deep in chemically induced slumber. Ellis did his best not to look at the faces behind the glass windows. While most were recognizable as human, a few weren't chambered until the infection had rendered them twisted masses of flesh and mottled fungal growth.

Despite the build up of body heat inside his suit, Ellis shivered. Eyes trained on the mop, he concentrated on the looped microfibers as they moved along the floor.

Soon, his shift would be over and the scientists in their white lab coats would arrive. That evening, while waiting in the cafeteria line, he'd heard a pair discussing research.

"Every subject in the last study died," said the silver haired woman. A younger man, ferret like eyes sharp behind glasses, shook his head. "That's why we use late stage patients in early human trials. Reversing effects in those cases will never happen, even with a cure. "

Ellis didn't know the scientists' names, and doubted they registered his presence. But the way they talked, like the people inside the boxes were lab rats, bothered him well into the final hours of his shift.

They *weren't* rats. They were still *people*.

Back at the front wall, Ellis returned the mop to its bucket. He glanced at the clock above the metal door. "Five minutes to spare," he said. Next to the clock, a domed emergency light protruded from the wall like a dead, bulbous red eye.

Gripping the cart handle, Ellis turned to wheel his janitorial supplies out of the room and banged a scrawny hip on a cryogenic chamber. "Dammit," he hissed, and rubbed his side. This chamber, he saw, was new and likely installed the previous day. He hadn't noticed it during the previous shift.

Against his better judgment, Ellis approached the glass and metal box, not so different from a coffin, and peered inside.

A young woman, still as a statue, lay beneath the chamber

window, hands folded neatly over her chest. Hair the color of raven's wings curled at the collar of white coveralls, but despite the bagginess of the clothing, Ellis saw a full, youthful figure underneath. He decided she was roughly his age, early twenties, with pale skin and lips the color of fresh blood.

The only evidence of infection, as far as Ellis could tell, were fine tendrils of filament escaping from one nostril, climbing in spider web patterns across the left side her face.

Ellis stood for several minutes, enchanted by her frozen beauty.

Suddenly, a loud bell chimed through the storage room, signaling a new hour and end of his shift. With much effort, Ellis tore himself away from the chamber and scanned his ID badge on the wall panel. The door whooshed open, and with one last, longing look over his shoulder, exited the room.

* * *

Following protocol, Ellis returned his cart and entered the decontamination showers. He stepped out of the biohazard suit, stripped off his uniform, and placed everything in a disposal bin. Then, with one, deep breath let the burning, hot water wash over his body.

Dried and dressed in street clothes, Ellis boarded the elevator and punched the button for surface level. As soon as the doors opened, dust assaulted his eyes, nose and mouth. Shielding his face with one hand, Ellis walked the short distance to his apartment.

Off to the east, a storm-muted dawn broke the horizon.

* * *

In the hours following, his mother's voice called out to him during restless, troubled dreams. She whispered a story to him, one from his childhood, about a princess under an evil witch's spell. A prince found her, preserved in a glass box, asleep as if in death. With love's first true kiss, the prince was able to wake the princess, and they lived happily ever after.

Ellis jolted up in bed, drenched with sweat and sheets tangled around his slim frame. A plan came to him, fully formed, and he quickly prepared for work.

* * *

Removing the glasscutter from the maintenance shop proved easier than expected. He slipped the tool into his janitorial cart and pushed it slowly to Storage Room 7 so as not to arouse suspicion. His heart thudded as he scanned his ID badge and entered.

Ellis completed the task of cutting out the chamber window efficiently, as efficiently as he sterilized the steel room's walls. With a burst of cold air, a smell rose out of the chamber, sickly sweet and fetid. For the first time in his life, Ellis felt a deep sense of accomplishment. She was more beautiful than any fairy tale princess, and he was going to save her. Gently, Ellis brushed filament from her icy mouth and lowered his face inside the box.

As he pressed his lips against the sleeping woman's, the red emergency light above the door began to flash.

Heather Santo is a procurement lead living in Pittsburgh,

PA with her husband and daughter. In addition to writing, her creative interests include photography, painting and collecting skeleton keys. Follow her on Instagram and Twitter @Heather52384.

The Garrison World by Dennis Mombauer

The transport touched down inside the bunker complex, and Fenton got off with the other recruits. The halls and corridors were endless, only partially outfitted with lights and ventilation, isolated from the planet's wastelands by gates that had been welded shut.

The veterans living here told Fenton that they had orders from Command to hold this position, and nothing else. None of them seemed to care about the condition of the bunker, about the derelict equipment and the vermin scurrying around.

* * *

Fenton learned the daily routines and discovered a lot of strange things about it. No one knew what the enemy looked like, and there hadn't been an attack for a long time—but occasionally, the bunker's surveillance systems indicated movement.

Fenton sprinted to an observation post, but could see nothing, even though the screens showed red dots approaching the closed gates and vanishing on contact. The veterans shrugged and grumbled something about glitches, and as Fenton couldn't find any hostile presence, he had no choice but to accept this.

* * *

It happened again, two more times—and after the second, one of the new recruits went missing in the remote hallways. The instruments marked an enemy that was nowhere to be seen… and if the bunker had been infiltrated, Fenton couldn't find any sign of it.

He asked the veterans for communication with Command, to which they only repeated their standing orders to hold position, resistant to all inquiries. Fenton organized patrols with some of the other newcomers, walking for hours along the dreary corridors, once again without noticeable results.

* * *

The alarms became increasingly frequent, and no amount of tinkering and reconnaissance could explain them. The immense bunker was under constant attack by incorporeal enemies, by a ghostly army that only the sensors could perceive—and with every wave, one of the recruits vanished.

Some of Fenton's comrades reported blurred forms moving through the corridors, found their belongings displaced or heard clanging sounds in the distance, and Fenton set up camp right in one of the surveillance rooms. The motion detectors reported movement in distant sections, then around them, finally inside the room—and everyone wondered if something alien stood right next to them.

* * *

Fenton gathered the remaining recruits and marched to confront the veterans, who never suffered any disappearances. The grizzled and stoic soldiers already came toward them in full armor. "New orders from Command. We are moving out, engaging the enemy. Grab your gear."

It was a long way to one of the gates not permanently welded shut, and it gave Fenton time to think, to become afraid. The entrance loomed large, and when it opened, he saw the planet's wastelands, as devoid of life as the bunker complex itself. Barren, and hungry.

After they herded out the recruits, the veterans closed the gates behind them, waiting for the next arrivals.

Dennis Mombauer currently lives in Colombo, Sri Lanka, where he works on climate change and as a writer of speculative fiction and textual experiments. He is co-publisher of a German magazine for experimental fiction, "Die Novelle – Magazine for Experimentalism," and has published fiction and non-fiction in various magazines and anthologies. His English-language debut novella, "The House of Drought," is coming out on July 14th, 2022, with *Stelliform Press*.

Homepage: https://dennismombauer.com/ / Twitter: https://twitter.com/DMombauerWriter

Daniel's Defense by Rachel Dempsey

If a bullet were to penetrate Sergeant Daniel Hutchins's skull in the middle of his forehead, creating a perfect cross-section of his brain, a neurosurgeon would immediately notice several signs of prior damage. Bruising from blunt force trauma, a hazing stunt gone wrong. Thiamine deficiency in the cerebellum due to prolonged alcohol abuse. Injured blood vessels and nerves pickled in excess dopamine and cortisol.

Likewise, if Hutchins ever agreed to let some pogue therapist pick apart his psyche, the warning signs would be hard to miss. But among the strongest men, the bigger the grief, the deeper they buried it.

On the surface, he was a model of American youth and vitality. Tall and muscled, with thick, shiny dark hair cut high and tight, and eyes his ex-fiancée had described as "the color of peaches drenched in raw honey." Her eyes were blue, webbed with red, those last few months on the screen. She'd stopped asking when his next planetary leave might be and while Daniel knew it was safer for her that way, the loss still ached. Not as much as the spot where they'd injected him, though.

Surely the medical scans will pick it up, Daniel had assured himself. Yet the alien implant must have fooled their primitive human technology, because he could still feel the microscopic device feasting on his brain stem. Controlling his body like some pubescent gamer with a favorite new avatar. He'd tried to cut the thing out, but they wouldn't let his hand press the blade deep enough. Burning, poisoning, drowning . . . they only let him go as far as agony, never death.

Though his medical retirement paperwork could take months or even years to complete, the Army discharged Sergeant Hutchins from Walter Reed National Military Medical Center on a bright day in early May.

A civilian. Days before his twenty-seventh birthday.

A veteran. Decades before he'd planned.

A weapon no one knew was coming.

He said goodbye to the thirty sick men in his warrior transition platoon—dead inside, every last one, robbed of their dignity and purpose. On the rarest occasion that the Army redeployed one of them, jealousy and resentment were prominent guests at the farewell party. As per the deal, Hutchins was going home, so his send-off featured goodwill and cake.

It was one of those rare, magical spring afternoons in D.C. when the April monsoons had passed but the bugs and stifling humidity had yet to arrive. After the drab palette of Martian deserts and hospitals, the colors of blossoms, lush grass and a cloudless sky seemed garish. Hurt his eyes. The light breeze smelled of lilacs. Grandma's front porch swing. How much more could he lose and keep advancing?

Traffic zipped up and down Wisconsin Avenue. Horns blasted; upbeat music blared out of open windows.

Was life always this loud?

Resting his sweating palms on his thighs, Daniel gulped for air. All around, in the middle of the day, people rushed . . . where?

What the hell do people do while they're waiting to die?

Not that they knew how soon the end was coming, like Daniel did. Reluctant to face his friends and family, he'd kept his release date to himself. His flight home wasn't until the following afternoon. He stood on the street corner with a duffel bag in his hand, looking right, left, then right again, when an old lady in yoga pants and a cream-colored tunic approached.

Just in time, he remembered to turn on his civilian-friendly smile. "Can I help you, ma'am?"

She chuckled. "I was going to ask you the same. You look lost."

"Yup," he said without thinking.

For an instant, he wanted so desperately to save this woman, to save them all, no matter how little they deserved it after the way they'd destroyed their species——no, that was them talking in his brain--he believed it might be possible. To stop.

"Where you trying to get to?" The old woman's gentle, raspy voice was soothing.

No fucking idea.

To the astonishment of both, Daniel started to cry.

Rachel Dempsey lives in Denver where she attends the MFA program at Regis University. Find her on Twitter @rachelsdempsey.

And Darkness and the Red Death Held Dominion by Lisa Short

I jumped out of the back of the truck; in my mind, I landed light as a cat, rifle steady in my hands. In reality, I thudded to the ground, barely keeping the rifle's muzzle pointed away from my own face. Baird saved me from being too embarrassed about that by catching his boot on the tailgate and pitching out headfirst right behind me. I grabbed the back of his Protective Mobile Test unit and yanked him upright with the help of another pair of hands—Inwood's, who winked at me before jogging away.

The rest of the squad gathered around the lieutenant. I quickly joined them, then glared at Baird until he did the same. "The objectives are about a mile northwest," the lieutenant was saying. "Look for any kind of shelter—a cabin, a shed, anything. Questions?"

"No, sir!" chorused the squad, with me belatedly chiming in *sir!* and Baird missing the cue entirely. I eyed him as we double-timed it into the woods, but he steadfastly avoided my gaze.

About ten minutes later, the lieutenant stopped us—at least, everybody else stopped, so I did too, but it was too dark for me to make out anything much past Inwood's shoulder in front of me. "Up ahead," somebody whispered. "A trailer."

"Portmanteau!" That was definitely the lieutenant. Our PMTs were set to respond only to the trigger word in his voice or our own; I guessed USAMRIID assumed that it sounded enough like PMT that we wouldn't forget it and that none of us would ever say *portmanteau* for any other reason.

Training kicked in and I shrugged the PMT straps off my shoulders and swung it around as the case broke open and clamped onto my chest, the twin compartments unfolding out and around my shoulders. The mask strips slapped lightly over my nose and mouth, pinching my nostrils shut; I barely felt the microneedles sinking into both sides of my neck. Once the PMTs activated, we had five minutes, exactly three hundred seconds, of ten-thousand-dollar viral immunity—I sprinted forward, right on Inwood's heels. We burst through the trees and I saw the trailer—rusted, listing, but there was a light in one of the broken-out windows—

Something hit my back like a sledgehammer. I flew forward off my feet, instinctively tucking my chin so that after one ass-over-teakettle rotation I ended up on my knees, rifle butt slapping into my shoulder as I snapped the sights up to my eye. My target's face swam into clear focus and I yanked my finger off the trigger in the nick of time. *Baird!*

I barely had time to feel relief that I hadn't capped my thus-far-unimpressive, three-week-long active duty career by blowing away a fellow soldier when Baird surged upright, off the ground where he'd presumably landed after slamming into me, raised his rifle, and fired point-blank at the back of Inwood's head. I screamed, muffled by the mask strips; beyond the glistening black ruin that was all that was left of Inwood's skull, several shadowy figures erupted through the trailer's sagging door and high-tailed it into the woods.

I didn't realize I was shooting at Baird until his chin snapped back and a jagged, fountaining gash replaced half his neck. The air shuddered with the staccato roar of massed rifle fire—having failed to meet the criteria for any possibility of containment, the squad was switching to plan B—B as in *backup,* B as in *bullets,* B as in *body bags*. I lurched forward on my knees, past Inwood who would never wink at me again to Baird, who was bleeding out in the mud.

The mask strips unpeeled themselves silently from my face, and his—our five minutes were over, and so was our retrieval operation. USAMRIID didn't need us to bring infected dead bodies back; they had plenty of those already. The lieutenant was already dropping incendiary disks onto the human-shaped humps in the trampled undergrowth. I sat back on my heels, staring down at the glassy eyes that used to be Baird and now were just lumps of tissue drying out in the smoky night air.

"Yes, it's wrong," I said to Baird's corpse. "But what else are we supposed to do? There's no cure, man. It's them or us."

The microneedles prickled my neck again and the clearing lit up like a Christmas light show, all of us flashing crimson as our PMTs' viral load test sequences engaged. A few green sparks had winked on already—if, every one of our PMTs shifted to green, the incendiaries would arm themselves with a ten-minute delay til detonation, and we'd beat feet back to the truck. If even a single one of us stayed red, or anyone tried to leave the clearing before all the test sequences had completed...well, the incendiaries would still arm themselves for detonation. They just wouldn't bother with the delay. I closed my eyes and rested my forehead against my knees, waiting for the end to come one way or the other.

Lisa Short is a Texas-born, Kansas-bred writer of speculative fiction. She is a member of the Horror Writers Association.

No Such Thing As Neutral by JM Williams

Self-destruct sequence initiated. Abandon ship!

The synthesized female voice bounced down the metal corridors like a thrown wrench. There was no way in hell Tyrese was going to let any godforsaken colonials have his ship. It was his first ship. It was his.

He checked the countdown. Nine and a half minutes left. Plenty of time to get to the escape pod and out a safe distance before the explosion. The last thing to do was to load as much of the medical supplies—the ones he was supposed to deliver to Carter Station—into the pod as possible before jumping.

Tyrese activated the ship's thrusters, sending it into a roll. That would slow down the pirates a bit. *Pirates. Bloody damn pirates.* The roll provided some artificial gravity, which allowed Tyrese to bear-crawl to the cargo hold. But when he arrived, he quickly found himself floating again. The ship shuddered and roared as the pirates had latched onto it and halted its rotation.

Self-destruct sequence deactivated.

Well, damn. Tyrese poked at the control panel for the escape pod, opening the door and checking the ship's systems. The pirates had hacked his ship, a faster and deeper intrusion than he had been expecting. Not only was the self-destruct system inoperable, the escape pod was locked.

That wasn't going to slide. He wasn't going to let some space thugs beat him. Not now, not ever. Tyrese activated the ships AI anti-hacking programs—the good, black-market kind—and increased the cabin's oxygen levels. Then he pulled himself down the corridor towards the engine room.

This was not his first run in with pirates. When the tempo of the war between the United Nations Government quickly went against them, Colonial Mars started paying privateers to attack non-colonial shipping. Even neutral ships were being attacked. Even neutral ships carrying medical supplies like the *Resonant.*

He had assumed it would be an easy job, had even marked his ship with the red crescent. Maybe that was what had made him a target. In times of war, meds were limited in supply and high in demand. But Tyrese was not averse to danger. He had been a fighter pilot with the UNG Navy for almost a decade. Pirate hunting had been his job then, before the war.

Tyrese didn't agree with this war. He was of the rare opinion that the colonials should have the right to choose. But then they threw their hat in with pirates. That was unforgivable. He'd seen people killed—wingmen and close friends—in pirate raids.

The only good pirate was a dead one, and he was determined to blow them all into the void. Ships and cargo headed to Carter Station were insured by the UNG, so as long Tyrese made it out alive, he could recover his losses.

Reaching the engine room, he ripped opened the rusted cover which housed the manual controls for the gas lines. He jerked the titanium lever to the side, bracing himself against a corner in the wall for leverage. Once he heard the satisfying hiss of hydrogen gas spilling into the corridors, he grabbed a filter mask from the safety cabinet and pulled it down over his face. Then he drifted back down to the pod.

Tyrese could hear the sound of the *Resonant's* side hatch being cut open. There wasn't much time left. He had to un-hack the escape pod and flee. The pod had "heavy-burst" thrusters designed to push the pod away from the ship as fast as possible. They would expend as much fuel in a few seconds as it would take to carry it all the way from Earth to the Moon in zero-g. Tyrese hoped the flame jet would ignite the hydrogen...

The ship groaned as its stubborn hatch was finally torn open. Tyrese hammered away at the console, trying to override the hack. He unlocked the escape pod controls and shut down the central computer. The lights in the corridor flickered off.

Flashlight beams and voices bounced around the corner leading from the entrance hatch. Tyrese sealed the pod door, strapping himself tightly into the only seat and entering the launch sequence into its control panel. Then he made a selfish prayer to Allah. He wasn't a religious man, but it never hurt to try. He knew he was on the right side of morality.

The pod lunged forward, shoving Tyrese back into the seat. He heard the brief roar of flame and felt a concussion of thunder, before entering the quiet vacuum of space. After a few shaky moments, the escape engines died, and he sat there motionless, feeling the drift. With a sigh of exhaustion, he put his hands to his face, thankful he was still alive. His fingers dripped slowly past the day-old stubble on his chin and back to their places at the pods controls.

Activating the pods maneuvering jets, Tyrese spun it around so the portholes looked upon the corpse of his ship. Any bits that could be identified as part of the *Resonant* were gone, as was a massive chuck of the pirate frigate which now drifted without power, away from the spreading debris.

Tyrese decided it would be best to ride the pod's momentum for a while before kicking in the drive engines and heading for Carter Station. He consoled himself with the thought that at least he wouldn't arrive there empty handed.

He had escaped, but at what cost? He had put a lot of his soul into that ship. What did it mean that it was so easy for him to let it go? A voice in his head told him he had done good, that sacrificing his ship had been worth it. But he didn't know where life would take him next. Maybe he should just surrender to the current.

Or maybe it was time to pick a side.

JM Williams is the author of dozens of SF/F books and stories. He serves as the Editor-in-Chief for Of Metal and Magic Publishing.

The View by Brett Anningson

It is a beautiful morning. Sun is shining, birds are singing, all is right with the world.

Ted yawned as he stepped towards the window, pulling back the faded blue shift to look out on the landscape of his dreams. This cottage was everything he and Alisa had worked for, dreamt of, and ultimately designed.

It was her skill at architecture that made it all possible. In an overcrowded world where wilderness was hard to find this cabin in Alaska was everything… and nothing.

"Wait" he mumbled to himself… "What the hell does that mean?"

Continuing in his head, Ted wondered what he was doing? Am I editing my thoughts? He ran his fingers through too short hair, thinning for some reason, and sighed, inhaling the wafting odour of vanilla and maple from the pancakes sizzling on the kitchen griddle.

"Alissa?" Ted called. But he did not turn from the window.

There was something else, an oily, mechanical smell. Steel, perhaps? This wasn't right. What had he meant when he said to himself that the cabin was nothing? There was something he was forgetting.

He turned towards the bedroom door. As Ted tried to open

it the wood shimmered, blurred, and became steel.

It came crashing back.

Ted was a pilot, a Fighter Pilot in the Terran fleet. He had crashed. He was captured. He was in prison.

Suddenly everything shifted and the cabin bedroom became the small metal cell imprisoning his darkening soul. He screamed… And screamed… And screamed.

Darkness.

It was a beautiful morning. Sun beamed through the blue curtains into the bedroom as Ted lay there listening. The fire was crackling, a pleasant noise that complimented the babbling of the brook winding its way through the backyard of this Alaskan paradise. A deep breath of clean mountain air cleared his head and made his stomach rumble. Alissa was cooking pancakes and he could hear her singing downstairs in the kitchen.

Humming along to her tune Ted's feet hit the pine floorboards as he turned towards the bathroom.

Wait, why was the bathroom in the bedroom? Hadn't it been at the end of the hall? His mind was still groggy with sleep, which must be the reason everything felt wrong. He must be remembering their old house in Colorado, near the spaceport, that was it.

The pancakes smelled so inviting and all thoughts of confusion left his mind as he revelled in Alissa's sweet voice.

Ted made it to the top of the stairs before the shift began. Looking down on her shadow, he called to his wife, somehow knowing that she would not answer. This wasn't real.

Which is when it hit him again, he was a prisoner, on Gratakk. He was a prisoner of war and this was a lie. What the hell was going on? Suddenly remembering the fear of yesterday Ted chose a different reaction, anger. The bastards had caught him after his ship had crashed and they had locked him in a cell promising "humane" imprisonment until his death. That was not going to happen. He was not going to spend his life in this tiny cell.

Pounding on the steel door he shouted his rage to the emptiness of his cell. "I won't forget! You bastards can't make me forget! I'll get out of here and kill you all!"

It was futile. Spent, he collapsed on the floor.

Darkness.

It was a beautiful morning. Sun is shining, birds are singing, all is right with the world.

Taking a deep breath Ted inhaled the glorious smell of his beautiful wife's pancakes. She had promised a treat for breakfast last night and he could not wait - Alissa's pancakes were a dream come true. He threw his feet to the pine floor, threw back the quilted comforter they had got as a wedding present and rushed down the stairs to her embrace.

Alissa smelled like heaven, vanilla, coffee, wood smoke from the iron stove, now this was what his dreams were made of. Ted twirled her in a dance across the room as she continued humming that beautiful tune that he just could not put his finger on.... what was it? When had he heard it last? Oh yeah, that morning in the cabin.

Which morning? This morning? Déjà Vu?

"Are you going to eat? Or just fish," Alissa asked playfully.

"You know I cannot resist your pancakes," Ted replied with a smile and sat down at the table, cradling the warm coffee mug in his hands.

He took a deep breath in and smiled. Life was perfect.

Fluffy barked to go out at the door and the mood was broken.

Well, not the mood so to speak, but the spell. For it was in that second that Ted realized fluffy was dead and had been for years. The sunlight faded to grey and another day in the cell began.

Darkness.

It was a beautiful morning. Sun is shining, birds are singing, all is right with the world.

Taking a deep breath Ted inhaled the glorious smell of his beautiful wife's pancakes. She had promised a treat for breakfast last night and he could not wait - Alissa's pancakes were a dream come true. He threw his feet to the pine floor, threw back the quilted comforter they had got as a wedding present and rushed down the stairs to her embrace.

Alissa smelled like heaven, vanilla, coffee, wood smoke from the iron stove, now this was what his dreams were made of. Ted twirled her across the room as she continued humming that beautiful tune.

"I have to eat quick," he quipped as he kissed her warm rosy cheek. "Fluffy and I are going fishing, and the fish are jumping."

With that, he tucked into the best pancakes he had ever tasted, drank his fresh brewed coffee, humming the tune Alissa had been singing as he took his pole from the wall.

"What a beautiful morning," he sighed, shutting the door and heading for the brook.

Brett Anningson has written over 1500 articles that have covered the gamut of every subject imaginable, writing about art, architecture, lifestyle, music, religion and society, He is a staff writer at Business View Magazine, co-authored, The Gnostic Gospel of Genesis and in his spare time writes witty and evocative Science Fiction.

They Think I Sleep by Andrew Swearingen

The comforting chill of the void has been replaced with tepid atmosphere and harsh lights, beating down on my shell.

All around, I sense them. The pink, fleshy bipeds, staring at me as their beam draws me into their craft. They stare up in awe...as they should.

The beam is released and I settle gracelessly onto the vessel's unforgiving floor.

The bipeds stir around me. They attempt to breach my shell, wishing to find me underneath. Their drills and beams have no effect on me. I feel them scan me with little devices. As they analyze me, I have done the same to them.

The warm blooded hominids are small, barely half as tall as my shell. Their bodies are frail. No armor or scales to protect them. They cover themselves with grey cloth, unsuited to protect them from any real threat. Much less from me.

Their feeble minds *can* comprehend that I am organic, which baffles them. Their fragile bodies cannot withstand the loving embrace of the void and thus have concluded that all life is incapable of living in the void. They attempt to read the etchings on my shell, given by my makers. But the bipeds language is too primitive to comprehend the iconography that encircles my shell from top to bottom. Their curiosity turns to a childish excitement. They have never seen anything like me.

One of the bipeds hypothesizes that I "hibernate". That I am asleep and pose no threat. I let them think I am asleep, ignorant of the fact that the destroyer of worlds is in their midst.

I stretch my senses further out. Their vessel is large, made up of dozens of room and hundreds of tunnels. I feel thousands of minds, scurrying about, obsessed with their small tasks. Energy hums through the ship powering the ship's engines, life support, artificial gravity, and weapons. Dozens of weapons' ports. This ship is built for war. To intimidate and oppress any challenger. I would need only moments to destroy all of it.

A new mind focuses on me.

A female, slightly taller than the rest of the rabble. She is attired in black, adorned with gold epaulets and medals. Her rigid, unforgiving thoughts focus on me, her gaze coursing greedily along the ridges of my shell. They cower and stutter in her presence. Simple drones meant to do her bidding. She is not simply their commander. She is their queen.

The queen cannot take her eyes off of me. She thinks I am a great discovery. She wishes to bring me to their home world so that she may be awarded with esteem and given another medal. She only aims to appease her masters. To make herself great in the eyes of others. But the drones see none of this. They see the façade of confidence. A mask of power.

Crushing this queen would bring such great satisfaction. My heart dances as I imagine opening my shell, reaching out my claws, and seizing her. To taste the queen's fear as she realizes just how little command she had over even her own small life, before crushing the pathetic shell that encloses her mind.

Then to move on to her drones, drinking in the terror as the leaderless minions flee in horror. Though they out number me by thousands, the ship full of primates are no match for me. I would crush them all, as I have to so many before them. As I did to my makers.

The queen turns her back to me.

I allow her to keep the illusion of power.

I have no reason to challenge her. Not yet. They will bring me to their world. Then I shall arise and taste their fear. They will bring me to their world, their... Earth, and I shall make it mine.

Andrew Swearingen has been published in multiple anthologies and loves writing stories about life, the universe, and (usually) time travel.

The Chill in his Bones by T. Fox Dunham

Garfield rubbed his arms and legs, trying to get warm. For two days they'd marched west into the Belgium frontier, deploying to block the surprise German advance. The cold gnawed through his coat, uniform, through his skin and down into his bones.

"You look like you're in outer space," Brooklyn Billy said. They fortified their fox hole with branches. Even in winter, water seeped into the hole, and Garfield carpeted the bottom with pine bundles so their legs wouldn't freeze.

"You're going to think I'm crazy," Garfield said. He hesitated but lacked a priest to confess to. "Right before the medics patched me up, I swear I saw angels. I must have died."

It had been two weeks since he'd returned to his unit after R&R in Paris, which was mostly a blur; in fact, he couldn't recall much of the last month since he'd been wounded and attributed his fuzzy recall to first the morphine in the military hospital and then the champagne at the Paris cathouse. Everything felt off but oddly familiar—the way you struggle to remember a dream after you wake. The last thing he remembered was blood squirting out of his neck after he'd caught a bullet from a German MG-42. A tall priest lumbered over him at the aid station and swung a rosary over him. He felt himself yanked out of his body. He could look down over the nurses. Aureate wings sprouted from their backs—alien angels. Extra eyes grew out on their faces. Then darkness crushed him, drowning him. He tried to scream but no couldn't open his mouth nor could he raise his hands to find it. The pressure of the blackness crushed him like he'd sunk to the bottom of the ocean.

"At least you went to heaven then," Billy said. "Could have been the other place with the lake of fire and dragons. Scares the shit out of me when I think about it."

"Doesn't scare me anymore," Garfield said.

"Oh yeah? Then what does?"

"This war never ending," he said. "I'd rather go to hell."

Artillery fired in the distance, pouring shells across the Belgium front where the German forces had mounted a winter counteroffensive, bulging out over Allied lines. Overcast skies grounded the P-51s, so it was up to the men on the ground to hold off the panzers and infantry. C company dug in outside of Dom Butgenbach with orders to slow the slow the German assault.

"Keep your eye on the ball," Billy said. Garfield aimed his rifle at a bunch of trees to the east, searching for Kraut infantry that got through the barrage. He listened for the grind of tank engines in the distance but all he heard was the sound of their breath on the background of howling wind. He rubbed at his body, his neck but couldn't get warm.

Green passed in front of a cracked birch tree that stood out in front of a patch of pine. Something looked off about them. He swore he'd seen their faces before. They moved weird, lurching forward, perhaps trying to get through a deep snow bank.

"Three," Billy said. "Two. One." They pulled their triggers.

Silver blood spurt out of the chest of the one on the left while Billy's grabbed his shoulder than ran for cover. Garfield fired again, but his target dodged out of sight. "I'm going after mine," Bill said.

Garfield got to his feet, stepping into the seeping water at the bottom of the foxhole. Water soaked through his boots but he didn't feel the chill. He felt . . . nothing. The German soldier leaped out of a pine tree and landed on top of him, knocking free his rifle. They wrestled, and Garfield smacked his head against a rock, cracking his skull. Somehow still conscious, he grabbed his knife off his belt and drove it through Fritz's eyes. The soldier screeched, stretching its jaw open like a snake swallowing a mouse. Then, his body went limp. Garfield checked felt the hole in his forehead and found black oil smeared down his palm. Words manifested in the air in front of his sight:

System Damage 63%...

System failure imminent...

Recall.

He passed out then woke up on a gurney in an aid station. A familiar priest waved a rosary over him. The beads glittered and pulsed.

"What are you doing to me?" Garfield managed to ask.

"Preparing you for transfer," the priest said. "Your backup memory preserved your core program." He spotted Billy on a table next to him. Sparks fired out of his open chest. His face wrenched in a frozen scream.

"It isn't heaven. This is hell."

"Hell?" the priest asked then drove a probe into Garfield's skull. "That's part of your primitive belief system. No. You're not in hell. But your soul is very much in tact; in fact, it's quite valuable. We've observed your species for many rotations of your sun. Your genetic code possesses a brutality and talent for conflict that we lack. Our enemy is an aggressive predator, and we are a peaceful kind."

"Just let me die," Garfield said.

"You're one of the lucky of your species," the priest said. "You would have died on Earth, shot in the neck at something you called the Battle of the Bulge. Our kind was there to transfer your neural patterns to pilot our weapons. You will never die."

Garfield's body seized, and he struggled against the weight of his limbs but couldn't get off the table.

"Don't worry," the priest said and traced a glowing silver circle in the air. "You won't remember any of this."

* * *

Garfield dug into the frozen ground, preparing his foxhole. He'd bundled up but ever since he'd been returned to his unit, he hadn't been able to get the chill out of his flesh and bones.

T. Fox Dunham is a cancer survivor and disabled author living in Lancaster, Pennsylvania with his wife, Allison. He's the author of the Philly crime novel Street Martyr, currently in development by Throughline Films, the author of many published short stories and his story Hermiod's Last Mission is canon for the Stargate Franchise, specifically Stargate Atlantis.

Following Orders by Kai Delmas

Private Rick Sherman, designation X9042, sat strapped into his seat in the Beta Squad shuttle. They were about to enter the atmosphere.

Which planet? What were they going to fight?

Questions he had to stop himself from asking. Otherwise the neural link in the base of his skull would chirp in his brain, reminding him to follow orders without question.

Though they were weightless since detaching from the cruiser, Rick couldn't help but feel rigid. Feet braced, arms tight, hands grasping the straps.

He could will himself to move. Might even be able to do it without the neural link interfering. He hadn't been ordered to sit like this after all. But what was the point?

His squadmates weren't doing anything either. They were quiet. Waiting for their next orders.

This was not what Rick had expected when he was drafted. The Federation's military vids always showed the soldiers laughing, having a good time. Always showed them victorious.

If one was false, was the other as well?

Private, ready yourself for atmospheric entry.

Now, Rick braced on his own accord. He could feel a clear down again. Real gravity after months in space.

Canon blasts erupted from below, making his heart hammer in his chest. They were heading straight into the action. He had known that. But he wasn't ready for it.

More canon fire. Their shuttle remained steady, on course. Ever downward, bringing them to the enemy.

Sweat dripped from Rick's brow, his hands were clammy. They could be shot down any moment. And then it would be over. Just like that.

Private, prepare for landing. Ready your weapon and charge. Shoot to kill.

The shuttle heaved into a level position, landing gear humming as it extended. They touched down with a thud and Rick's straps unclipped.

His squadmates jumped out of their seats and readied their weapons as the landing doors began to open.

Private! Move!

Rick stood up and grabbed his weapon, not on his own. He stepped in line with his squad and readied himself for the doors to open all the way. Shots were already being fired.

He wasn't ready for this. No, he couldn't do this.

He willed his feet to stand still.

Private! You will follow orders! Move! Shoot to kill!

Rick's body moved as it should, heading out of the shuttle with his squad. Shots ricocheted off the metal of the ship, pinged off armor and lodged into flesh.

Rick was surrounded by screams of fury and pain. He didn't even realize he was shouting himself, firing his weapon, running for cover.

Red dust and red rocks were everywhere. He hid behind a large boulder, breathing heavily, blood pumping in his ears.

Only now did he realize he was in control of his body again.

A moment of respite granted by the neural link.

And in that moment he scanned the battlefield to see who it was they were fighting.

They were human. Like him. Why were they fighting other humans from the Federation?

Follow orders, Private! Shoot to kill!

Rick's grip stiffened on his gun as he raised it to fire at the enemy. He willed his finger to freeze.

Were they really the enemy? Why was he supposed to kill them?

Follow orders, Private!

His finger squeezed involuntarily. The bullet went straight into a man's chest. His arm swiveled to the right and his finger squeezed again. And again.

Why was he doing this? Why were they fighting?

The neural link was in complete control now. Rick could only watch in horror as his body moved like an expertly trained soldier. He watched as he killed enemy soldiers, one after another.

If only he could close his eyes to make it stop.

Rick hammered his will against the power of the neural link to no avail. His body was no longer his own.

It was following orders and would continue to do so until the Federation was victorious.

Kai loves creating worlds and magic systems. His fiction is forthcoming in Martian and Tree and Stone. His Twitter: @KaiDelmas

STEP...TOUCH...JOURNEY...HUNGRY. by Colton Long

The first time the monolith spoke to me, guttural and growling, spitting out words like it despised the taste of them in its no-mouth, I figured it was one of my squad playing a little joke on the comms.

"STEP...TOUCH...JOURNEY...HUNGRY."

There it was again, same four words as before. It was a shit joke, since the words were nonsense, and how can you laugh at a joke when you can't make sense of it?

But the third time the monolith spoke, I knew it couldn't be one of my Marines. No human vocal cords could conjure such a voice: metallic, eerie, a faint undercurrent of metal scraping against flesh. Chills burrowed into my body, through my airsuit, my underclothes, my skin, and deep into my cybernetically reinforced bones.

I ground my feet into the soil of this desolate moon and barked, "Squad, on me!"

Hanna snapped to my side. "Sergeant?" She peered through her LSR-45 assault rifle's holosight as puffs of moon-dust rose beneath her boots, ethereal clouds of golden brown slowly melding into the infinite black of the cosmos.

I pointed a gloved finger at the thirty-foot-tall pillar of

looming stone. "The monolith is talking."

Lowering her rifle, Hanna cocked her head at me. "You space-sick again, Sa'id?"

"On any other day, tell me straight and true that I'm losing my wits, and I'll believe you, but that monolith *spoke* to me."

"Only thing talkin' on this dry moon is you, sir…and now me."

On my left-hand flank, Alister padded forward, jabbing his rifle's muzzle at the monolith.

"**STEP! TOUCH! JOURNEY! HUNGRY!**" boomed the monolith.

Alister jerked backward, as if he'd touched a live wire. Hanna flinched, eyes bulging so wide I thought they might tumble out of their sockets. "Ok, *now* the monolith is talkin'," she whispered.

Trevin, who'd been guarding our rear, flung himself into the vanguard, sliding his vast bulk between me and the monolith. "It's a damn trick," he growled over his shoulder. "Told you as much when Command sent us down here to eyeball this…*thing*. There are insurrectionists in the system, ya? Bet you the insurs hid a communicator behind the monolith and rigged some explosives."

The stone monstrosity said nothing, as if it too was contemplating Trevin's theory.

With hand signals, I ordered Alister to flank the monolith. He crouch-walked to the left, rifle raised, giving it a wide berth.

Trevin pointed his miniature railgun at the silent stone. "That's how the insurs would do it," he said. "Monolith starts chattering, we go all sorts of curious, have ourselves a little look-see, and…BOOM. You know insurs love a good bit of trickery."

My headset crackled. "Strong theory," said Alister's voice, "but it's as false as false can be. Fire up your Geo-Scan, and you'll see what I see: nothing. There's not a thing hidden behind the monolith. Or in it. It's as solid as Trevin's belly." The man in question grunted his annoyance.

I tapped my temple, switching on my own helmet's Geo-Scan. "Holy hellfire."

"What?" asked Alistair.

"Look *down.* I can't even see the base of the column...it's...it's beyond our scans' range. Someone sunk the monolith *into* the moon. Miles deep, maybe penetrating even into the bloody core."

"**STEP CLOSER**," thundered the monolith suddenly. Between the metallic growls, I heard notes of hesitance, as if it hadn't quite grasped our tongue. As if our language was alien to it.

"The surface is so smooth," murmured Alister over the comms. "Like glass."

"**TOUCH ME.**"

My headset crackled. Alister again. "The stone glimmers... ripples..."

Gooseflesh rose on the nape of my neck. "Alister, don't touch it!" I'd lost a hundred and fourteen Marines to the insurs. A hundred and fifteenth would break me. "Alister?"

"*AH!*" Silence. Then, "I've gone inside," said Alister's voice, only it wasn't. It was a recreation, a poor approximation of what something else *believed* his voice sounded like. "It's warm but cold. Not-warm but not-cold. Cold...cold...**COLD**."

My headset crackled, and *something* lunged through the static. Not-warm but not-cold tendrils reached through my earpiece and tunneled into my ear. I screamed.

Before me, Trevin dropped to his knees, clutching his helmet—and as if someone had pulled on an invisible string, he was yanked into the monolith, vanishing into the glimmering, rippling stone.

"Hanna, call—" Tendrils slid down my skull, riding veins and nerves, and *clamped* my lips shut. In the sliver of time before they climbed into my eyes, I watched Hanna's shrieking face vanish into the monolith. Up came the tendrils, spilling into my irises, and all turned to gleaming black.

"**IT HAS BEEN A LONG JOURNEY**," bellowed the monolith. It wrapped itself around my ankles and dragged me into stone. But it wasn't stone. It was worse. It was malevolent. Living, thirsting, hungry.

And with my final thought, I grasped the cold, black enormity of the monolith's message: "**STEP CLOSER. TOUCH ME. IT HAS BEEN A LONG JOURNEY. AND I AM HUNGRY**."

By day, Colton Long writes political attack ads. By night, he writes speculative fiction. Find him on Twitter @ColtonM-Long.

Head Start by Liam Hogan

"Damned thing's armoured!" Sarge roared as she tumbled into my dugout, somewhat singed. The problem with being the platoon's only radio operator was that I had HQ in one ear and Sergeant "Mad Dog" McGinnly in the other. It was my job to relay information between them. Mostly, that was repeating whatever the army boffins said; I reckon the whole sector and beyond could hear McGinnly's profanity-laced views.

"Only to be expected." The calm reply conjured images of a pipe and a cosy fire, both tauntingly attractive right now. "Instruct your men to shoot it in the head."

"The head?" I echoed.

"Sticky-up bit. Like an overturned flower pot? Packed with cameras and other sensors. You can't miss it."

The nanowarrior was twenty-feet tall and the turret was about half the size of an average human head. So not a particularly large target, but with everyone shooting at that one point, (even if most of us *did* miss it,) it didn't take long for a shot to ring home.

The mechanical leviathan went over like a ton of lead bricks, rattling the ground as we whooped and hollered. The break-away nanotech had been heading for the Olsen mine, rich in both iron and silica, perfect conditions to breed up a whole swarm of nanites to replace the loses the AI enemy had suffered on the main front. Normally, we'd have waited for it to get cosy and then dropped a big ol' bomb (or a small nuke, same difference) on both mine and robot, but the steep-sided valley the works sat in was where the colonists had sheltered when the fighting had begun. They'd be slaughtered unless we halted the nanowarrior in its tracks.

So the boffins had given us a new strategy and new weapons to carry it out, our bullets rich in neodymium. The rare-earth magnets would disrupt the forces that kept the nanobots together. At least, that was the theory.

I hadn't expected it to be *this* easy.

But, even as I clicked the radio to report the glad tidings, there was another flurry of gunfire and the answering scream of a plasma bolt. Shortly after, McGinnly was hot and heavy in my ear again. "It regrew!" she screamed.

"What regrew?" the boffins and I asked at the same time.

"The damned head! Damn thing is unstoppable!"

"Keep shooting, Sergeant."

"That's *it*?" she yelled in dismay as I relayed the instructions. "Is that all you've damned well got?"

"Shoot it in the head," the boffins said with infinite patience. "And if it grows another, shoot *that* as well."

Huddled at the fringes of the action I trained my scope over the earthworks. Again, the warrior went down, but this time the troops didn't cheer. They, and I, watched, horrified, as a new head took shape, in about the same time it took for the dust to clear. As soon as it lumbered to its heavy feet, we hit it again.

It became almost a game, the two section leaders competing

for who could knock it down fastest. It seemed to take a little longer to get to its feet each time, which ought to have cheered us I guess, but often as not it would pop up with a different weapon than before. Flamethrowers, needle darts, mortars, or just the old standard, duel plasma cannons. A real Swiss Army knife of lethal destruction to keep us on our toes, its hivemind AI doing its best to adapt and overcome.

At some point, and it was hard to tell how long it had been planning the manoeuvre, the nanowarrior found refuge in one of the many caves that edged the ravine in which we'd set our ambush. Now, each time it went down, it regrew that damned head in private. It took a few knockdowns after that for me to notice—"It's getting smaller!"

"Of course," came the voice in my ear, though I hadn't realised I'd left the radio on. "It's a nanowarrior. Not, technically, one warrior at all, but thousands—millions—of them. Each time you blow off the head, it repurposes more of itself to regenerate—"

"—so eventually, it'll run out of nanites?"

"Precisely. Do pass the word along, there's a good fellow."

"Thought as much," grunted the Sergeant, looking rather less frazzled. She grabbed my spare magazine and told me to make myself useful. So I crouched in the trench with the rest of them as we plugged away. In short order, the nanowarrior was human height, and then half, such that the head looked almost natural, and then it began to look cartoonish, though, as Rodriguez found to his cost and embarrassment, no less dangerous. He won't be sitting down for at least a month.

Finally the thing that scuttled back into its hole didn't bother to emerge and Sarge, chewing the risk of going in after it, ordered us to collapse the cave roof.

We sat around for an hour and then left a few automated

defences (perilously close to enemy tech in McGinnly's opinion) that would instantly destroy anything bigger than a lapdog and then shipped out, job done.

It was almost sunset and we were back on base and celebrating the day's deeds, when one of the left-behind sensors was tripped. The remote camera was offline by the time we got to a monitor and we had to wind the feed back to see what had done the offlining.

A black tide of over-turned flower pots on spider legs flowed over the ground in front of the collapsed cave, our dumb guns silent as they were engulfed. Just before the camera was briefly mirrored in a dozen inquisitive nanotech lenses and the feed went dead, we watched the tide divide, two rivers flowing in opposite directions.

One, heading towards the benighted colonists and the mine, rich with raw materials.

And the other…?

The other was headed straight for us.

Liam Hogan is an award-winning short story writer, with stories in Best of British Science Fiction and in Best of British Fantasy (NewCon Press). He's been published by Analog, Daily Science Fiction, and Flame Tree Press, among others. He helps host Liars' League London, volunteers at the creative writing charity Ministry of Stories, and lives and avoids work in London. More details at http://happyendingnotguaranteed.blogspot.co.uk

Printed in Great Britain
by Amazon